THE EXTRAORDINARY FILES

Spider Invasion

Paul Blum

RISING★STARS

It is th... ...de.'

nasen
Helping Everyone Achieve

nasen

NASEN House, 4/5 Amber Business Village, Amber Close,
Amington, Tamworth, Staffordshire B77 4RP

Rising Stars UK Ltd.
22 Grafton Street, London W1S 4EX
www.risingstars-uk.com

Text © Rising Stars UK Ltd.
The right of Paul Blum to be identified as the author of this work has
been asserted by him in accordance with the Copyright, Design and
Patents Act 1988.

Published 2007
Reprinted 2008

Cover design: Button plc
Illustrator: Enzo Troiano
Text design and typesetting: pentacor**big**
Publisher: Gill Budgell
Project management and editorial: Lesley Densham
Editor: Maoliosa Kelly
Editorial consultant: Lorraine Petersen

British Library Cataloguing in Publication Data.
A CIP record for this book is available from the British Library.

ISBN: 978 1 84680 183 9

Printed by Craft Print International Limited, Singapore

CHAPTER ONE

The helicopter landed. Parker and Turnbull got out.
They were British Secret Service agents on an
important mission. They had lots of bags with them.

The helicopter had landed at P3, a military base, high up in the Welsh mountains. It was a good place to hide a new weapon of mass destruction. The new weapon was called 'Tiger Claw'.

Agents Parker and Turnbull were met by Major Stephens. He was P3's commander.

"I'm glad you're here," said Major Stephens. "We need your help. First, you need to see the film we've made of what's going on here. I cannot watch it with you. I find it too upsetting."

The major turned away sadly. The agents could see the tears in his eyes.

Turnbull and Parker watched the film. They saw spiders crawling around the main building of P3.

Then they saw soldiers fighting the spiders. They sprayed gas at them but they couldn't kill them.

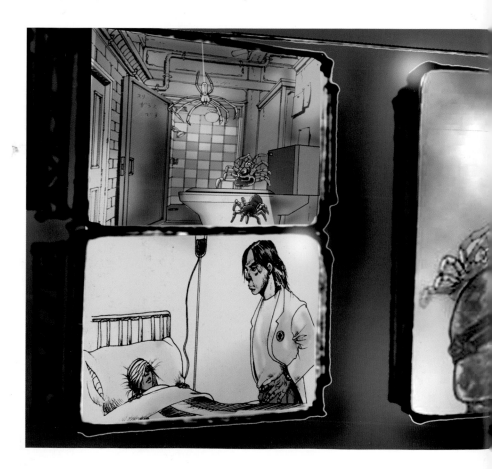

The spiders stuck to the soldiers' clothes. The soldiers were screaming and running away.

Then they saw the major's 11-year-old son, Georgie. He was very ill in bed. When he coughed, spiders came out of his mouth. His bed was covered with them. They saw why the major could not watch the terrible film.

The major came back when the film was over.

"How is Georgie now?" asked Turnbull.

"He's very weak," said the major.

"Do the spiders come from him and only him?"
asked Parker.

The major nodded his head. "They seem to grow in him and then hatch. The doctors want to send him home to have tests but MI5 say that he is a security risk and must stay here."

Parker looked at the major. "Are you a brave man, Sir?" he asked.

"I am," said Stephens. "But I am frightened to see my boy like this."

Parker took a deep breath. "Have you heard of alien abduction, Major?"

"I don't see what the spiders have got to do with alien abduction," said the major.

"Aliens need a human to live in. They need a safe place to hatch. Your little boy Georgie might be that safe place," said Parker.

Major Stephens put his head in his hands. There were tears in his eyes again.

Turnbull said quickly, "Of course there may be other reasons for Georgie's problem. That's why we need to do some tests. You must not panic."

The major looked up. "I'm not panicking but I am very angry. When your son is very ill and the government tells you that he cannot go home for treatment, you feel angry."

The agents nodded.

"We'll set up our equipment and see Georgie," Turnbull said.

Major Stephens shook Turnbull's hand. "Thanks for coming," he said. "I'm glad you are here."

CHAPTER TWO

As soon as they were alone, Turnbull told Parker off. "Why did you upset that poor man with all that alien abduction stuff?" she demanded.

"It's part of our brief," he said.

"But can't you see what a terrible state Stephens is in?"

"Look, Agent Turnbull, we've got a difficult job on our hands here."

"Agent Parker, Major Stephens' son is very ill and in danger. He needs a bit of cheering up right now."

Parker smiled. "Hang on a second, Laura. Remember this is MI5 not a family counselling service."

"Don't start telling me off, Agent Parker. The most important thing about this job is handling people well."

"Maybe," he muttered.

They started to unpack their bags. Parker unpacked a computer and medical equipment. Turnbull unpacked her clothes.

Parker unpacked tools and survival rations.

After five minutes Parker exploded.

"I don't believe this!" he shouted angrily. "You have the cheek to tell me what this job's about. I've brought all the useful equipment and you've brought your wardrobe."

"Oh yes, and what is so useful about a hunting knife, a diver's torch and tins of spam?" Turnbull replied.

"And I suppose there's going to be a fancy-dress ball so you'll need all those clothes."

"Shut up, Parker. I need to look smart and professional at all times. Besides, I need things to cheer me up while I'm here," said Turnbull. "And don't forget I'm the boss here, Parker. *I* decide what *I* want to wear!"

Parker grinned. He bowed to her. "Yes Captain. You command and I will obey."

"Good," she said. "Let's go and see Georgie."

CHAPTER THREE

Georgie was in bed. He was very pale and thin.
He tried to smile. He coughed and two spiders landed
on his pillow.

"Georgie, we are going to do some tests on you,"
Turnbull said kindly. "We think we can make you
better."

"I wish I could die, Agent Turnbull. Look at all the trouble I am making."

"It's not your fault, Georgie. We will make you better," Parker said smiling.

They gave Georgie an injection to put him to sleep. Then they put Parker's 'Alien 2' scanner onto his chest. Parker peered through his powerful microscope.

"You did well back there, Robert," said Turnbull. "You made the boy feel better."

"Thanks, Laura. But I think I might have spoken too soon. Look at the slide." He put it up on the computer. Turnbull looked at it.

"The one on the left is the DNA of all spiders. The one on the right is the DNA of Georgie's spider," Parker said.

"So what does that mean?" said Turnbull.

"Georgie's spider is an alien life force."

Turnbull sighed. "You were right, Parker – this could be an alien abduction."

Parker looked into the microscope again. "The question is do these aliens kill their host?"

Four days went by. Georgie was getting weaker and weaker. Parker did more tests on the spiders. He found out that the spiders seemed to take energy from the computers they sat on.

"They seem to be feeding off our computers," he told the major.

"The spiders are also breeding quickly," said Turnbull. "It may only be a question of hours before they break out of the area you have shut them in. Then they will be all over the camp."

The major shuddered. "I have been given my orders. We must abandon P3 when that happens. We will take the Tiger Claw missiles with us. The base will be bombed." He sobbed. "My orders say that Georgie must stay here. I shall give him strong sleeping pills so he will not suffer long."

Parker and Turnbull were silent. There was nothing to say. They felt sorry for the major as they watched him spend his last hours with his young son.

CHAPTER FOUR

That night at ten o'clock Rufus arrived. He was taken straight to Major Stephens. The major called for the two agents immediately.

"Who are you?" asked the major. "How did you get here?"

Rufus smiled but he did not reply. He was a big man. Over seven feet tall. He had long, red hair and a long, red beard. He had a strange look in his eyes.

"I'll ask you again. How did you get here? There are no roads to this base. P3 is not on any maps," said the major.

"My name is Rufus," said the tall stranger. "I have come to help you."

"Help us with what?" asked Parker.

"Help you get rid of the spiders."

Everyone was silent.

"How do you know about the spiders? Who are you?" said the major.

But Rufus just laughed. "You do not have time to hear my life story. I say again. Do you want me to get rid of the spiders?"

The major nodded his head.

"It will cost a lot of money," said Rufus.

"It's yours."

Rufus smiled again. "Take me to the spiders," he said.

They unlocked the big steel doors of the base. There were thousands of spiders all over the machines. Rufus went into the room. He pulled a strange object out of his bag and put it in his mouth. Parker wondered if it was a missile but it was a musical pipe.

A beautiful tune came out of it. One by one, the spiders followed Rufus in a long line.

He walked slowly out of the camp. The soldiers and their families could not believe what they were seeing. Rufus took the spiders down to the lake. All the spiders jumped in and were drowned.

"Well, he's certainly earned his money," said Parker.

"I suppose he has," said Turnbull. But deep down inside she felt uneasy.

When Rufus came back to P3, he was a hero. The soldiers carried him on their shoulders. They were about to have a celebration party when the doctor rushed in.

"Georgie is having a fit," he shouted. "Come quickly, Major."

They rushed to Georgie. The poor boy was shaking. He could not stop coughing.

The major was in a panic. He was frightened that he was about to lose his son. "Doctor, give him an injection so that he can sleep," he begged.

"His heart is too weak, I can't risk it," the doctor replied.

Suddenly Rufus came into the room. "Stand aside," he said. He went up to the bed and felt Georgie's head. Then he took out his pipe and played a tune. The music filled the room. It hung in the air like magic dust.

Georgie stopped coughing. His eyes closed and he fell into a deep sleep.

The major shook Rufus' hand. "You have powers," he whispered. "Thank you."

"Georgie is still very sick," said Rufus. "We must see how he feels when he wakes up."

"So can you stay at P3 and make him better?" asked Major Stephens.

Rufus paused. "I will," he said, "but only if you make me a promise."

Rufus took Stephens aside and whispered to him. The major looked shocked but after a few seconds he nodded his head and said, "I promise."

CHAPTER FIVE

Georgie had a deep sleep. When he woke up, he looked a lot better. The next day, the colour was back in his cheeks. Two days later, he was eating again. Five days later, he was back at school and playing with the other children.

Parker and Turnbull were talking to Major Stephens when Rufus came in.

"It is time for you to keep your promise to me," he said.

The major blushed. "I should not have made that promise," he said. "I cannot keep it now. It's not within my power to promise so much money as a reward. But if you stay at the base I am sure that my government will give you a medal for what you have done."

Rufus shook his head sadly. "You have let me down and you will pay for it." He picked up his bag and left.

The camp was quiet again. The spiders had gone and Georgie Stephens was better. Parker and Turnbull got ready to leave.

"I don't feel right about this case," Turnbull said.

"I don't think it is finished yet," replied Parker. "The major didn't keep his promise and there is going to be trouble."

"Do you think this is still a case of alien abduction?" Turnbull asked.

Parker nodded. "The alien is still out there. He is not far away and he hasn't got what he wants yet."

That night, all the people at the base went to Georgie's 12th birthday party.

Everybody was happy and thankful that he was well again. His father, Major Stephens, lit the candles on his cake.

"Ladies and gentlemen. Let's wish Georgie a very happy birthday."

"Happy birthday, Georgie," said lots of voices.

"Happy birthday, Georgie," said one more deep voice.

The major's mouth dropped open. Rufus had suddenly appeared at the table. Some of the soldiers tried to grab him but he stopped them with a wave of his hand. "I've only come to take what is mine," he said.

Then he pointed at Georgie. "12 is a wonderful age to be," said Rufus. He put his hand into his pocket and got out his pipe. "Hands up all the children in the room," he said. 50 little hands shot up. "Do you believe in magic?" he shouted.

"Yes," they replied, laughing.

"Then listen to my little tune," he said.

Parker saw what was happening. He threw himself across the table and landed in the birthday cake. "Stop him!" he shouted.

The pipe music filled the air. One by one, the children got up from the table and followed Rufus. Georgie led the way. They followed him to the gates of P3. The soldiers tried to grab him but they could not move their arms. Turnbull tried to karate kick Rufus but her foot would not move from the floor.

Everybody was frozen. Time seemed to stand still.

Rufus led the children to the side of a mountain and they all disappeared into it.

Then the music stopped and the adults could move again. They rushed to the mountain. They hammered at the stone with their fists. But there was no way in.

The children had gone!

CHAPTER SIX

London Vauxhall MI5 Headquarters

Parker and Turnbull were back at MI5 Headquarters. Parker gave his report to Commander Watson. "I think what happened at P3 was an alien abduction," he said.

Commander Watson smiled. "What do you think, Turnbull?" he asked.

"I don't know, Sir."

"Well," said the commander. "Maybe Rufus was an alien from another planet. But he may just have been a criminal who kidnapped children to get ransom money."

"Has he asked for money yet?" asked Parker.

Watson looked out of his office window at the River Thames.

"Not yet," he said slowly, "but we will be ready for him when he does."

"Why do you think the children followed the pipe music?" Parker asked.

Watson smiled at him. "Come on, Parker. You must know the fairy tale of the Pied Piper."

"Of course I do."

"Then you know that there has always been magic in the world. This is not the first time this has happened and it probably won't be the last."

Commander Watson looked through some books on his desk. "You know, Parker, we keep cases like this in the Extraordinary Files until we can get some real answers."

Parker felt uneasy. He thought that Commander Watson knew a lot of things that he wasn't telling them.

Parker and Turnbull went for a drink in a café.

"You're very quiet," Turnbull said after about 15 minutes. "What's bugging you?"

"I don't like cases that end like this," Parker replied slowly. "I want to know who Rufus was. I want to know what happened to all those children. I feel sorry for their poor parents."

"That's not like you, Parker. You are getting soft in your old age," smiled Turnbull.

Parker could not get the P3 case out of his mind.
For months he looked for clues to do with the missing
children. He was just beginning to forget the case when
a strange thing happened. He was walking his dog in
Hyde Park. He found himself watching a football match
between two teams of children. Suddenly his heart
started to beat very fast. Georgie Stephens was one
of the goalkeepers!

He followed the children back to their school. And there was the biggest surprise of all! The class was full of the missing children from P3. He went up to the gates and used his binoculars. He felt a shiver run down his back. There were two teachers in the staffroom. He felt dizzy as he looked at them. One looked like Turnbull and one looked like him!

Parker did not tell anybody what he had seen.
He knew that what had happened at P3 was even
stranger than he had thought. He began to have
a terrible dream over and over again. It was such a
terrible dream that he woke up screaming in a cold
sweat. In the dream he and Turnbull had followed
Rufus and his magical pipe music. They had followed
him into the mountain where they had fallen into
a deep sleep.

Could it be that the two teachers he had seen
in the school were the real Parker and Turnbull?
If this was true, then what had happened to
Agents Robert Parker and Laura Turnbull at P3?
Were they part of a terrible experiment that had
taken away their lives? Had they become just
another case in the Extraordinary Files?

GLOSSARY OF TERMS

abduction kidnapping

alien creature from another world or outer space

breeding multiplying

brief instructions

counselling to give advice about problems

hero a person who has done something incredible and worthy of respect

kidnapping stealing children

microscope an instrument with a lens that magnifies small objects so that they can be seen

ransom money requested as payment for return of something

rations portions of food

Secret Service Government Intelligence Department

shuddered shook with horror

QUIZ

1 Where was the P3 military base?

2 What was 'Tiger Claw'?

3 Who was in charge of P3?

4 Where were the spiders coming from?

5 What age is Georgie?

6 Who arrives at the base?

7 What musical instrument does Rufus play?

8 How does Rufus get rid of the spiders?

9 Where does Rufus take the children?

10 Who does Parker see in Hyde Park?

ABOUT THE AUTHOR

Paul Blum has taught for over twenty years in London inner-city schools.

I wrote The Extraordinary Files for my pupils so they've been tested by some fierce critics (you!). That's why I know you'll enjoy reading them.

I've made the stories edgy in terms of character and content and I've written them using the kind of fast-paced dialogue you'll recognise from television soaps. I hope you'll find The Extraordinary Files an interesting and easy-to-read collection of stories.

ANSWERS TO QUIZ

1 In the Welsh mountains

2 A new weapon of mass destruction

3 Major Stephens

4 They were coming from Georgie,
   Major Stephen's son

5 11

6 Rufus

7 The pipe

8 He plays the pipe and the spiders follow him
   down to the lake where they drown

9 He takes the children inside a mountain

10 Georgie